P9-DBS-826

Jack and Annie have opened a door to a world of literacy that I know will continue throughout the lives of my students.—Deborah H.

Through your books, my students have been taken to a higher reading level.—Olga V.

Thank you for writing good books for young children. Your attention to historical details and inclusion of accurate science information make these books a wonderful learning resource. Perhaps, most of all, I appreciate your invitation to read and read and read some more. Lifelong readers are born! Hallelujah!—D. Wright

Dear Readers,

One snowy day in Connecticut, I wished I could escape to a sunny island. I was far too busy to take a vacation, so I took a trip in my imagination. That's how I began working on this book about Hawaii.

In my research, I learned that the islands of Hawaii are even more beautiful than I had thought. They began as volcanoes that rose from the sea. Over millions of years, birds and wind brought seeds to the masses of rock. In the perfect climate of the Pacific, trees, flowers, wildlife, and insects thrived. When people discovered the islands, they were amazed by the natural wonders they saw.

This is a big reason why I love being an author so much. By using my imagination, I can go <u>anywhere</u> I want. I can escape the cold weather and feel the fresh, sweet-smelling air of beautiful faraway islands. Wherever you are right now, whatever the season, I hope you'll use your imagination to escape to Hawaii, too.

Aloha!

Mary Pope Osborne

MAGIC TREE HOUSE® #28

High Tide
in Hawaii

by Mary Pope Osborne

illustrated by Sal Murdocca

SCHOLASTIC INC.

New York   Toronto   London   Auckland   Sydney
Mexico City   New Delhi   Hong Kong   Buenos Aires

For Mel and Dana

No part of this publication may be reproduced in whole or in part,
or stored in a retrieval system, or transmitted in any form or by any means,
electronic, mechanical, photocopying, recording, or otherwise,
without written permission of the publisher. For information regarding
permission, write to Random House Children's Books,
a division of Random House, Inc., 1745 Broadway, 11th Floor, New York, NY 10019.

ISBN 0-439-54014-3

Text copyright © 2003 by Mary Pope Osborne.
Illustrations copyright © 2003 by Sal Murdocca. All rights reserved.
Published by Scholastic Inc., 557 Broadway, New York, NY 10012,
by arrangement with Random House Children's Books, a division of Random House, Inc.
SCHOLASTIC and associated logos are trademarks
and/or registered trademarks of Scholastic Inc.

21   8 9/0

Printed in the U.S.A.   40

First Scholastic printing, January 2004

MAGIC TREE HOUSE is a registered trademark
of Mary Pope Osborne; used under license.

Contents

Prologue

One summer day in Frog Creek, Pennsylvania, a mysterious tree house appeared in the woods.

Eight-year-old Jack and his seven-year-old sister, Annie, climbed into the tree house. They found that it was filled with books.

Jack and Annie soon discovered that the tree house was magic. It could take them to the places in the books. All they had to do was point to a picture and wish to go there. While they are gone, no time at all passes in Frog Creek.

Along the way, Jack and Annie discovered that the tree house belongs to Morgan le Fay. Morgan is a magical librarian of Camelot, the long-ago kingdom of King Arthur. She travels through time and space, gathering books.

Jack and Annie have many exciting adventures helping Morgan and exploring different times and places. In Magic Tree House Books #25–28, they learn the art of magic. . . .

1

A Ship?

Jack and Annie were sitting on their porch, reading books. Jack was reading about gorillas. Annie was reading about Pilgrims.

Suddenly Annie closed her book. She looked up into the sunset.

"Hey!" Annie said with a smile.

Jack looked over at her.

"*It's back!*" she said, jumping up.

"Oh, man," breathed Jack. He knew she was talking about the magic tree house.

Annie could always tell when it was back.

Jack closed his book and stood up.

"We're going to the woods!" he called through the screen door. "There's something we have to check on!"

"Be back before dark!" their mom said.

"We will!" said Jack.

He picked up his backpack. Then he and Annie headed across the yard. When they got to the sidewalk, they started running. They ran up their street and into the Frog Creek woods.

In the last light of day, they hurried between the trees. Finally, they came to the tallest oak. They held their breath as they looked up.

The magic tree house *was* back.

"Good going," said Jack.

"Thanks!" said Annie.

She started up the ladder. Jack followed. It was nearly dark inside. But the sun-dried wood smelled like a summer day.

"What kind of special magic will we look for this time?" said Jack.

They glanced around the tree house. They saw the scrolls they'd brought back from Shakespeare's theater. They saw the twig from the mountain gorillas and the pouch of corn seeds from the first Thanksgiving.

"There!" said Annie. She pointed to a book in the corner. A piece of paper was sticking out of it.

Jack picked up the book. Then he pulled out the paper and read:

Dear Jack and Annie,

Good luck on your fourth journey to find

a special magic. This secret rhyme will
guide you:

> *To find a special magic,*
> *build a special kind of ship*
> *that rides the waves,*
> *both high and low,*
> *on every kind of trip.*

> *Thank you,*
> *Morgan*

Jack looked at Annie.

"A ship?" he said.

She shrugged. "Yep. I guess we have to build a ship. Where do we go to build it?"

She and Jack looked at the book's cover. It showed palm trees, a beach, and a beautiful ocean. The title was:

A VISIT TO OLD HAWAII

"Oh, wow!" said Annie. "I *love* Hawaii!"

"How do you know you love it?" Jack asked. "We've never been to Hawaii."

"Well, we're going now!" said Annie. She pointed at the cover. "We wish we could go there!"

The wind started to blow.

The tree house started to spin.

It spun faster and faster.

Then everything was still.

Absolutely still.

2

Aloha!

Jack opened his eyes. A gentle wind brushed against his skin. It smelled sweet and fresh.

Annie looked out the window. "Nice!" she said.

Jack looked out, too. The tree house had landed on top of a tall palm tree. The palm tree was at the edge of a flowery meadow.

On one side of the meadow, a cliff dropped down to the beach and ocean. On the other side of the meadow were the rooftops of a small village.

Beyond the village were tall gray mountains. Misty clouds hid their peaks. Waterfalls gushed down their sides.

"I *told* you I loved Hawaii!" said Annie. "Don't you?"

"I have to learn about it first," said Jack. He pushed his glasses into place and opened their research book. He read aloud:

> Hawaii is a chain of islands in the Pacific Ocean. The largest island is Hawaii, which gives its name to the whole group. The islands were formed millions of years ago by volcanoes. The volcanoes erupted under the

ocean. Over time, their craters rose
above the water.

"Wow," said Annie. "We're on the top of a
volcano."

"Yeah," said Jack. He read on:

The volcanic rock crumbled and
turned to soil. Over millions of years,
wind and birds dropped seeds on the
islands. Plants and trees began to
grow, and birds and insects made
their homes.

"Cool," said Jack. He took out his notebook and pencil and wrote:

wind and birds brought seeds

He read some more:

About two thousand years ago, people

**first came to Hawaii. They came in
canoes from other islands in the
Pacific. They rowed for thousands of
miles across the ocean, guided only by
the wind and stars.**

"Hey, listen," said Annie.

Jack put down the book and listened. Sounds of music and laughter floated on the breeze.

"There must be a party in that village," said Annie. "Let's go."

"What about building that ship?" asked Jack.

"We'll figure that out later," said Annie. "Let's meet some people at the party. Maybe they can help us."

She started down the ladder.

Jack heard a whoop of laughter in the distance. *The party does sound fun*, he thought.

He packed up his things and followed Annie down to the ground.

The sun was low in the sky. They walked through the meadow toward the village. Everything was bathed in a golden red glow.

"Oh, man," breathed Jack.

There was beauty everywhere: purple flowers shaped like bells, white flowers that looked like stars, tall, feathery ferns, green spiky plants, big orange-and-black butter-flies, and tiny yellow birds.

When they got close to the village, they saw an open area filled with people. Jack and Annie slipped behind a palm tree. They peeked out at the party.

There were about fifty people, including grown-ups, teenagers, and little kids. They were all barefoot and wore wreaths of flowers around their necks.

A woman was chanting. Her words rose and fell like waves. She chanted about a volcano goddess named Pele.

While she chanted, other people played music. Some blew on pipes that looked like flutes. Others shook gourds that sounded like baby rattles. Some hit sticks together to make clicking sounds.

Most of the villagers were dancing to the music. They stepped from side to side. They swayed their hips and waved their hands.

"They're doing the hula," whispered Annie. She smiled and waved her hands, too.

"Don't get carried away," whispered Jack.

He took out their book and found a picture of Hawaiians dancing. He read:

The early Hawaiians had no written language. They told stories with hula

**dancing. The hula is a blend of
dancing and chanting poetry.**

Jack pulled out his notebook. He started a list about early Hawaii:

no written language

stories with hula

Suddenly Jack heard loud laughter and clapping. He looked up. Annie was gone!

Jack peeked out from behind the tree. Annie was doing the hula with the dancers! But no one seemed surprised. Everyone just smiled at her as they kept dancing.

A girl caught sight of Jack. She looked about Annie's age. She had long, shiny black hair and a big, friendly smile.

"Come do the hula!" she called to him.

"No way," Jack breathed.

He slipped behind the tree again. But the girl danced over to him and took his hand.

"Join us!" she said.

"No thanks," said Jack.

The girl didn't let go. She pulled Jack into the open. The music got louder. The dancers and musicians nodded and smiled at Jack.

Jack stood still. He didn't know how to do *any* kind of dance, let alone the hula! He stared at the ground, clutching his backpack and notebook until the music and dancing ended.

The Hawaiians gathered around Jack and Annie. They all had friendly, open faces.

"Who are you?" the young girl asked.

"I'm Annie," said Annie. "This is my brother, Jack."

"I'm Kama," the girl said. "This is my brother, Boka." She pointed to a boy in the crowd who looked about Jack's age.

The boy stepped forward. He grinned a big grin just like his sister's. He pulled off his wreath of red fluffy flowers. He put it around Annie's neck.

"A *lei* to welcome you," Boka said.

Kama then pulled off her lei and put it around Jack's neck.

"*Aloha*, Jack and Annie!" everyone said.

3

Sleepover

"*Aloha*," said Jack and Annie.

"Where did you come from?" a pretty woman asked.

"Frog—" Annie started.

But Jack broke in. "From over the mountains," he said quickly. He pointed at the mountains looming in the distance.

"We are glad you have come to visit us," the woman said.

Everyone smiled and nodded.

They're all amazingly nice, Jack thought.

The music started again. As people began to dance, Kama took Annie's hand.

"Sit and talk with us," she said.

She and Boka led Jack and Annie to the edge of the clearing. They sat cross-legged in the grass. Kama picked up a wooden bowl. She held it out.

"Please eat," she said.

"What is it?" asked Annie.

"It is *poi*," said Kama. She scooped some poi out of the bowl and licked it off of her fingers.

"You eat it with your hands? Cool," said Annie. She stuck her fingers in the bowl and licked off the poi. "Mmm . . . good."

Jack stuck his finger in the bowl, too. The gooey mixture felt like peanut butter. But when he licked it off his finger, it had a weird taste—both bitter and sweet.

"Hmm," he said, but he made a face.

"He doesn't like it," Kama said to Boka.

"No, no," said Jack. "It's . . ." He tried to think of something polite. . . . "It's very interesting."

Kama and Boka giggled. Then they stuck their fingers in the bowl and ate some poi.

"Interesting!" they exclaimed. They cracked up laughing. Jack and Annie laughed with them.

"Now tell us about your home over the mountains," said Kama, "this place you call 'Frog.'"

Kama's friendly smile made Jack want to tell her the truth.

"It's actually called Frog Creek," he said. "It's very far away—much farther than just over the mountains. We traveled here in a magic tree house."

Kama's and Boka's eyes got huge. They smiled even bigger smiles than before.

"That sounds fun!" said Kama.

"You are so lucky!" said Boka.

Jack and Annie laughed.

"Yeah, we are," said Jack. He felt great telling their new friends about the tree house. He and Annie had never talked about it with their friends back home.

"Can you stay here tonight?" asked Kama.

Jack shrugged. "Sure, we can stay at least one night," he said.

Kama hurried over to the pretty woman. They spoke together for a moment. Then Kama returned to Jack and Annie.

"Our mother invites you to sleep at our house," she said.

"Great," said Annie. "Thanks."

Jack and Annie stood up. In the gray twilight, they followed Kama and Boka through the village. They wove between small huts with steep roofs until Kama stopped in front of one.

"This is our house," she said.

The hut had no door—just a wide entrance that opened into one large room.

Kama and Boka led Jack and Annie inside. In the dim light, Jack could barely see the dried-grass walls and the woven-grass mats on the dirt floor.

"Where do we sleep?" he asked.

"Here!" said Boka.

He and Kama lay down on the mats. Annie pulled off her lei and shoes. Then she lay down, too.

"Oh," said Jack. "Okay."

He took off his shoes and wreath of flowers. He used his backpack as a pillow when he lay down. The warm wind rustled the palm leaves outside. Music drifted in from the party.

"The ocean is calling," said Kama.

Jack could barely hear the waves in the distance.

"Tomorrow we will take you wave riding," said Boka.

"You mean *surfing*?" said Annie.

"Yes," said Kama.

"Cool," said Jack. But he wasn't sure he meant it. Surfing actually seemed pretty scary.

Kama seemed to hear his thoughts. "Don't worry," she said. "We'll have fun."

"No kidding," said Annie.

Soon Jack heard steady breathing. The other kids had fallen asleep.

Oh darn, we forgot to ask them about building a ship, he thought. *I guess we'll have to do that tomorrow. . . .*

Jack closed his eyes and yawned. Soon he, too, was fast asleep.

4
Garden Paradise

Jack heard pounding noises. He imagined Boka and Kama were building a ship.

He opened his eyes. Only he and Annie were still in the hut. A piece of cloth covered the doorway. Jack sat up and shook Annie.

"Wake up!" he said.

She opened her eyes.

"I think they're building a ship outside," said Jack. "Come on, let's go."

Annie jumped up.

"Don't forget your lei," she said.

They put on their flower wreaths. Jack lifted the cloth over the doorway, and they stepped out into the warm sunlight.

Boka, Kama, and their parents smiled at Jack and Annie. They were all working. But no one was building a ship.

Boka was pounding a wide strip of bark with a wooden club. Kama was using a stone to pound something that looked like a fat sweet potato. Their parents were weaving grass mats.

"What are you making?" Jack asked.

"I'm making *tapa*," said Boka. "First I beat the bark of the mulberry tree into thin sheets. Then my father pastes the sheets together to make cloth for us."

"This is the root of a *taro* plant," said

Kama. She pointed at the squashed white vegetable. "When you add fruit to it, you get poi."

"Great," said Jack. "By the way, do you ever build ships?"

"Ships?" asked Boka. "What for?"

Jack shrugged. "To sail away?" he said.

"Why would we do that?" asked Kama.

"Good question," said Jack, smiling.

"Can I help?" Annie asked Kama.

"Sure," said Kama. While she showed Annie how to pound the taro root, Jack slipped back into the hut. He pulled out his notebook and quickly added to his Hawaii list:

tapa—bark pounded into cloth

taro root—pounded for poi

ship—?

Jack heard Kama ask her parents if they could play now.

"We've finished our chores," said Kama. "May we take Jack and Annie to the ocean?"

"For wave riding," said Boka.

Jack held his breath. He half hoped their parents would say no.

"Yes, go have a good time with your friends," said their father.

"Come on, Jack!" Annie called.

Jack put his notebook away. He pulled on his pack and joined the others outside.

"We'll be back in a little while," said Kama.

"Don't forget to eat breakfast!" said her mother.

"We won't," said Kama.

Where will we get breakfast? wondered Jack.

He and Annie followed Kama and Boka. They passed villagers hard at work. Some carried firewood or water. Others were cutting grass or stripping bark from trees. Everyone smiled and waved.

"Hungry?" Kama asked Jack and Annie.

"Sure," they said.

Kama and Boka went into the grove of

palms near the huts. They climbed up two slanting tree trunks, using their hands and feet to push themselves up. At the top, they shook the palm leaves.

"Watch out!" Kama shouted.

Jack and Annie jumped back as big, round coconuts fell to the ground.

Kama and Boka slid down the trees. They each picked up a coconut. Then they found rocks and began to whack the hard shells. They whacked and whacked until their coconuts cracked into halves.

Kama shared hers with Annie. Boka shared his with Jack.

Jack drank the fresh, sweet milk inside the coconut. "Mmm!" he said.

"Interesting?" asked Boka.

"No. *Mmm* means *good*!" said Jack.

Everyone laughed.

Then Kama picked bananas off a banana tree and gave them to Jack and Annie. Jack peeled his and took a bite. It was the best banana he'd ever eaten.

When breakfast was over, they all headed into the flowery meadow. The sky was the bluest blue Jack had ever seen. The grass was the greenest green. The flowers and birds sparkled like jewels.

Hawaii is like a garden paradise, Jack thought.

He wanted to look up Hawaiian birds and flowers in the research book. As the others kept walking, he stopped and pulled out the book.

"Jack! Come look!" Annie shouted. She was standing at the edge of a cliff with Boka and Kama.

Jack put away the book and hurried to join

the others. He looked down at a beach fifty feet below.

There were no people. Only seashells and seaweed lay on the glistening white sand. Big, foamy waves crashed against the shore.

"Wow!" said Annie.

Uh-oh, thought Jack.

5
GO!

Boka looked at Jack and grinned.

"Ready?" he asked.

"I'm ready!" said Annie. "Where do we get our surfboards?"

"Down there," said Kama. She pointed to a rocky path that led to the beach.

"Let's go," said Annie.

Annie, Boka, and Kama started down the path. Jack followed, moving slowly and carefully.

When he stepped onto the beach, Jack slipped off his shoes. He dug his toes into the dry, warm sand. It felt as soft as silk.

"Actually, I wouldn't mind just taking a walk on the beach," he said to the others.

But no one seemed to hear. They had all walked over to a row of wooden surfboards propped against the rocks.

Boka picked out a long board and lugged it over to Jack. "For you," he said.

Jack took the board and looked up at it. It was as tall as his dad.

"Isn't this a little *big* for me?" he asked.

Boka shook his head. He chose a board for Annie. Then he and Kama grabbed a couple for themselves.

Jack took a deep breath. "I'd like to read a little about surfing first," he said. He put his board down and pulled out the research book.

"What is *that*?" asked Kama.

"It's a book," said Jack. "It tells you about things."

"How does it talk?" said Kama.

"It doesn't talk," said Annie. "You read it."

Kama looked confused.

"Jack, forget the book now," Annie said. "Let's just do what Boka and Kama tell us." She headed for the ocean, lugging her board.

Jack sighed and put the book away. He left his pack in the sand, picked up his board, and followed the others.

They all stopped at the edge of the water.

"First we need to get past the breaking

waves," said Kama. "Then we'll show you what to do next."

Together they waded into the cool, shallow water. *The waves don't seem all that big,* Jack thought hopefully.

But as he waded deeper into the ocean, the breaking waves began to look bigger and bigger. When the first wave hit him, Jack leaned against it, lifting his board. He nearly fell over.

Kama, Boka, and Annie moved farther out into the ocean. Jack watched as a wave loomed over them. They all threw their boards over the wave and dove into it.

Jack struggled forward. The next time a big wave came toward him, he threw his board over it. Holding his glasses tightly, he ducked under.

When Jack stood up again, he wiped the water from his eyes and glasses. His surfboard was close by. He grabbed it before another wave came.

Jack kept fighting his way forward. By the time he got past all the breakers, the water was up to his chest.

"We'll paddle out to catch a big wave!" said Boka.

Jack frowned. "But—"

"Don't worry, Jack," said Kama. "It will be fun!"

Boka and Kama pulled themselves onto their boards. They lay on their bellies and began paddling with their hands out to sea.

Jack and Annie lay down on their boards, too. Paddling over the gentle waves, Jack relaxed. Now, *this* was something he could do all day.

"When I say *go,* paddle fast back toward the shore!" said Kama.

"When do we stand up?" said Annie.

"When you start toward the shore!" said Boka. "Stand up with one foot forward. Stretch out your arms to keep your balance!"

"But don't try to stand up the very first time!" said Kama. "Just ride your board on your belly!"

"I see one coming now!" said Boka.

"Wait, wait!" said Jack. Everything was happening too fast. He had questions.

"*Go!*" Kama shouted.

Jack saw a big wave rolling toward them. Before he knew it, Boka, Kama, and Annie were paddling quickly toward the shore. Jack paddled like crazy to keep up.

Suddenly the wave lifted him and swept him forward! Jack zoomed toward the shore with amazing speed. Out of the corner of his eye, he saw Boka and Kama—*and* Annie!—all standing up.

Jack wanted to be like them. In a flash, he went up on his knees. He put his left foot forward and stood up! For one second he felt like a soaring bird—then he lost his balance!

Jack fell into the water, grabbing his glasses just in time. The wave crashed down on top of him! Water filled his mouth and went up his nose. His board and his lei were swept away.

Jack twisted and turned in the churning water. When his head bobbed up above the water, he choked and coughed.

Another big wave crashed down on him, and he went under again. When he came up, he plunged forward, desperately trying to get to shore.

Again and again, Jack was thrown down and slammed by breaking waves. But each time, he got up and hurled himself closer to shore.

Finally, Jack dragged himself out of the ocean. Feeling bruised and battered, he fell onto the sand.

6

Shake-up

"Jack!" cried Annie. She ran to him. "Are you okay?"

Jack just nodded. He put on his wet glasses. He felt shaky and mad at himself. *I never should have tried to stand!* he thought.

Kama picked up Jack's surfboard from the shallow water and brought it over to him.

"I told you not to stand," she said, laughing. "You fell hard."

It's not funny, thought Jack. *I nearly drowned!*

"The best thing to do is to go right back out," said Boka.

"You go," said Jack. His eyes and nose burned from the salt water. "I'll stay here." He walked over to his pack, picked it up, and took out the research book.

"Come on, Jack!" said Annie. "Try it again! Stay on your belly this time!"

"No, this time I'm going to *read* about surfing first," he said.

"Aw, you should just try it again," said Annie. "Not *read* about it!"

She ran to him and pulled the book out of his hands. Jack jerked it away from her. He slipped and fell onto the sand.

Kama and Boka laughed again.

"Why are you laughing?" Jack snapped. "You don't even know how to read!"

Boka and Kama looked hurt.

"Jack!" said Annie. "That was mean. Say you're sorry."

Jack opened his book and pretended to read it. He *did* feel sorry, but he was too upset to say so.

"Fine, stay here," said Annie. She went back to Boka and Kama. "Let's go."

As Jack sat alone on the beach, he looked up from his book. He watched the other kids paddling through the water.

"I don't care," he muttered. "I'm *never* going back out in those waves."

Morgan didn't send us here to surf any-way, he thought. *She told us to build a ship. But how the heck are we supposed to do that?*

Jack heaved an angry sigh. Now he was cross with Morgan. He turned to the back of the book and searched the index for "ship."

Suddenly Jack heard a rumbling from under the sand. The ground started to shake. It shook so hard, the book flew out of Jack's hands!

Jack bounced up and down on the beach. Shells were jumping up and down, too. Rocks tumbled down from the cliff.

It's an earthquake! thought Jack.

The rumbling stopped.

The shaking stopped.

Jack looked around. Everything was normal again, except some rocks rolled around at the bottom of the cliff.

Jack looked out to sea. Kama, Boka, and Annie were past the breakers. They were sitting on their surfboards, laughing and talking.

Everything seemed okay. But Jack felt

sure that something was wrong. He grabbed the Hawaii book from the sand. He looked up "earthquake." He read:

> Earthquakes in Hawaii have been known to cause tsunamis (soo-NAH-meez), which used to be called "tidal waves." An earthquake can cause water out at sea to be set in motion. The water grows higher and higher as it moves toward land. Just before the tsunami strikes, water may pull away from the shore. Then it returns in a gigantic wave that crashes over the land and washes everything away.

Oh, man! thought Jack. *A tsunami might be coming!*

7

Ride for Your Lives!

Jack had to find out more about tsunamis quickly. He read as fast as he could:

> A tsunami can strike a few hours—or a few minutes!—after an earthquake. It depends on the strength of the earthquake and where it took place. After earthquakes, it is safest for islanders to seek higher ground.

We have to get to higher ground now! thought Jack, dropping the book.

He ran down to the edge of the ocean. Boka, Kama, and Annie were still paddling out beyond the waves. Jack forgot all about their fight.

"Hey, you guys!" he yelled.

They didn't hear him.

Jack went into the shallow water. "Hey, you guys!" he yelled. "Come back!"

They still didn't hear him.

Jack ran to his surfboard, grabbed it, and ran into the ocean. He fought the breaking waves. Once he was past them, he threw himself on his board and paddled wildly.

The wave swells grew as he paddled. He could hardly see Annie, Boka, or Kama over them. Jack paddled faster and faster, trying to reach them.

"Hey!" he yelled. *"Hey!"*

Boka looked back at him. He gave Jack a friendly wave, then turned away again.

I have to get them to come to me! Jack thought frantically. "HELP! HELP!" he yelled at the top of his lungs.

The three kids jerked around. They paddled quickly toward Jack with worried faces.

"What's wrong?" Annie cried when they got closer. "Are you in trouble?"

"We *all* are!" said Jack. "A tsunami might be coming! There was an earthquake when I was on the beach!"

"We'd better ride in fast!" said Boka.

"Stay on your bellies!" said Kama. "It's safer!"

"Here comes a wave!" cried Boka.

They all started paddling.

The swell of the wave picked them up.

They were all swept forward!

Jack gripped the sides of his board as he zoomed along with the others. Suddenly he dropped down as the wave curled under. It felt like a roller coaster! But he stayed on his board as the wave carried him to shore.

Jack rolled off into the shallow water. He snatched up his board and ran onto the sand. Boka and Kama were waiting.

"Good riding, Jack!" said Boka.

"Where's Annie?" asked Jack.

Boka pointed. Annie was in the shallow water, pulling her board in. As they watched, something very weird began to happen to the ocean.

The water around Annie started to pull away.

8

The Big Wave

"Run, Annie!" Jack screamed.

The water drew away from the beach, and a loud hissing sound came from the sea.

Suddenly fish flopped on the bare sand!

Annie threw down her board and ran. She grabbed Jack's hand as she ran by him. Jack grabbed Boka's hand, and Boka grabbed Kama's hand. They all ran together, pulling each other along as they raced to the cliff.

Boka and Kama ran up the cliff path. Jack

and Annie grabbed their shoes and Jack's pack. Then they scrambled up the path, too.

At the top of the cliff, everyone looked back. Jack couldn't believe his eyes!

A wave was rising up like a dark mountain of water. It came surging toward the shore, growing even taller!

"Wow," whispered Annie.

"Get back!" shouted Boka.

The four of them bolted back from the edge of the rocky slope. The mountain of water crashed against the cliff. Water sprayed over the top of the rocks and rained down on them.

When the water rolled back over the cliff, they all hurried back to the edge to see what had happened.

The rocky cliff path was gone. The gigantic wave was moving back out to sea, taking rocks, sand, seaweed, seashells, and the surfboards with it.

"Scary," breathed Annie.

"Yeah," said Jack. "We just made it."

"Boka! Kama!" voices yelled.

They turned around. Jack saw Boka and

Kama's parents racing across the meadow toward them. Other villagers followed.

The two Hawaiian kids ran into their parents' arms. Soon Jack and Annie were surrounded by villagers. Everyone was laughing and crying and hugging each other.

Jack hugged Annie. He hugged Kama and Boka and their parents—and lots of other people he didn't even know.

9
Telling the Story

Finally, the hugging and crying and laughing died down. The villagers started walking back to their huts.

Jack and Annie followed Boka, Kama, and their parents.

"We felt the ground shaking," said Boka and Kama's father. "We knew a big wave might follow!"

"Jack saved us!" said Boka. "He read in a book and found out about the big waves."

"What's a book?" asked his mother.

"Show them," Annie said to Jack.

Jack reached into his pack and took out their research book.

"It tells about the big waves in here," he said. "Books give lots of information."

"Ah," said Boka and Kama's mother. "A book is a good thing."

"Books tell stories, too," said Annie.

"That is impossible," said Kama. "The book cannot move its feet or wave its hands. It cannot sing or chant."

"That's true," said Jack, smiling.

"Now we should do the hula," Boka said to Annie, Kama, and Jack, "and tell our story."

"I'll watch," said Jack, stepping away.

Boka and Kama's father called for music.

The villagers gathered around. A man

started to play a pipe. A teenage boy knocked two sticks together. Some women began shaking rattles.

Boka, Kama, and Annie waved their hands in time to the music. They stepped from side to side. They swayed their hips.

Kama chanted about going out into the water. She, Boka, and Annie waved their hands to show how they paddled out to sea.

Kama chanted about how Jack had warned them. She and the others waved their hands to show how they rode their surfboards to shore.

Then Jack surprised himself. He waved his hands to show how he rode his surfboard like a bird soaring through the air. The next thing he knew, he was stepping from side to side. He was swaying his hips. He was doing the hula!

Kama chanted about how the water had pulled away from the shore—and how they had climbed to safety—and how the giant wave had crashed against the cliff.

As Kama chanted the story, all the villagers joined in the dance. The tall grasses swayed. The palm trees swayed. And all the hula dancers swayed, too.

When the story ended, everyone clapped.

"Thanks for helping us," Boka said to Jack and Annie.

"We're a good team," said Annie.

"We are best friends," said Kama.

"Yeah," said Jack. "I'm sorry I said mean things."

"We're sorry we laughed at you," said Boka.

"I'm sorry I grabbed the book," said Annie.

"Our mother says friendship is like riding the waves," said Kama. "Sometimes you ride low, gentle waves. Sometimes you ride high, rough ones."

Annie gasped. She looked at Jack. She repeated Morgan's rhyme:

To find a special magic,
build a special kind of ship
that rides the waves,
both high and low,
on every kind of trip.

"*Friend*ship! That's the ship!" said Jack.

"And we built it!" said Annie.

She and Jack burst out laughing.

Boka and Kama looked a little confused, but they laughed, too.

"We have to go back to our own home now," Annie said to Boka and Kama.

"It's time to say good-bye," said Jack.

"We never say good-bye," said Kama. "We say aloha when we greet our friends. And we say aloha when we leave them."

"Friends are always together," said Boka,

"even when they are far apart."

"Have a good journey in your magic tree house," said Kama.

"Thanks," said Jack and Annie. They waved to all the villagers. "*Aloha!*"

"*Aloha!*" everyone called back.

Then Annie and Jack started through the meadow. Tiny yellow birds and orange-and-black butterflies flitted about them.

At the edge of the meadow, they came to the grove of palm trees. They climbed up the rope ladder into the tree house.

Out the window, Jack saw the tall mountains, the small village, the flowery meadow, and the ocean. The water was peaceful again.

"I still have my lei," said Annie.

She took it off. Though the red flowers were wet, they were still a little fluffy.

"It's proof that we found the special magic," said Jack. "The magic of friendship."

Annie put the lei on the floor next to the play scrolls, the twig, and the corn seeds. Then she picked up the Pennsylvania book.

"Ready?" she asked.

Jack sighed. "I love Hawaii," he said.

"*Finally*, you admit it," said Annie. She pointed at a picture of the Frog Creek woods. "I wish we could go home now."

The wind started to blow.

The tree house started to spin.

It spun faster and faster.

Then everything was still.

Absolutely still.

10

Everyday Magic

Jack opened his eyes.

The sun was setting beyond the woods. No time at all had passed in Frog Creek.

"Welcome back," said a soft, lovely voice.

Morgan le Fay was in the magic tree house.

"Morgan!" cried Annie. She threw her arms around the enchantress.

Jack hugged Morgan, too.

"Look, Morgan," said Annie. "We have proof we found four special kinds of magic!"

"Yes, I see," said Morgan.

Morgan picked up the play scrolls that Shakespeare had given Jack and Annie in old England.

"You found the *magic of theater*," she said.

Morgan picked up the twig from a mountain gorilla in the African cloud forest.

"And the *magic of animals*," she said.

Morgan picked up the pouch of corn seeds from their trip to the first Thanksgiving.

"And the *magic of community*," she said.

Finally, Morgan picked up the wreath of flowers from Kama and Boka.

"And you discovered the *magic of friendship*," she said.

Morgan looked at Jack and Annie for a long moment. "Listen carefully to what I'm about to tell you," she said.

"Yes?" They both leaned forward.

"You are now Magicians of Everyday Magic," said Morgan. "You have learned to find the magic in things you encounter on earth every day. There are many other forms of everyday magic. You never have to look far to find it. You only have to live your life to the fullest."

Jack and Annie nodded.

Soon you will be called upon to use your knowledge of Everyday Magic in the realm of fantasy."

"The realm of fantasy?" said Jack.

"Are we going back to Camelot?" said Annie.

Before Morgan could answer, a shout came from the distance. "Jack! Annie!"

"Our dad's calling," said Annie.

"You must go home now," said Morgan gently. "Rest—and get ready to test your powers. Your most exciting challenges are yet to come."

"Good-bye, Morgan," said Annie and Jack.

They hugged the enchantress. Then Jack took the Hawaii book out of his pack and gave it to Morgan. He put on his backpack and followed Annie down the ladder.

When they stepped onto the ground, there was a great roar above them. Jack and Annie looked up. A swirl of sparkling light lit the top of the tree.

Then the light was gone. The tree house was gone. Morgan le Fay was gone, too.

Jack and Annie didn't speak for a long moment. Then Jack broke the silence.

"Our most exciting challenges are yet to

come?" he said. "What do you think Morgan meant by that?"

"I don't know," said Annie.

"It sounds a little scary," said Jack

"That's okay. We can handle it," said Annie. She smiled. "We're *Magicians of Everyday Magic.*"

Jack smiled. "Yeah," he said. "I guess we are."

They walked out of the woods as the sun was setting. Down the street their mom and dad were standing on their front porch. They waved at Jack and Annie.

Jack felt a surge of happiness. *There's another kind of everyday magic,* he thought, *the magic of family.*

In that moment, it seemed the best magic of all.

HAWAII TIMETABLE

Millions of years ago, volcanoes rose from the Pacific Ocean to form the islands of Hawaii.

Around 1,500 years ago, Polynesians came to Hawaii. They were the first people to discover the islands. They traveled over 3,000 miles in wooden canoes from other islands in the Pacific.

In 1778, an Englishman named Captain James Cook made the first recorded European visit to Hawaii.

On August 21, 1959, Hawaii became the fiftieth state of the United States.

Today, over 6 million tourists from all over the world visit Hawaii every year.

MORE FACTS FOR
JACK AND ANNIE AND *YOU*!

Tsunamis were once called "tidal waves." Scientists no longer call them that because the waves have nothing to do with tides.

The Pacific Tsunami Warning System alerts the public of earthquakes or other disturbances that take place at sea. It puts out warnings on radio and TV. Sirens may also sound warnings. The warnings alert people to stay away from beaches and move to higher ground.

When the first Polynesians arrived in the Hawaiian islands 1,500 years ago, they brought the custom of riding surfboards with them.

According to one ancient Hawaiian legend, hula dancing began when Pele, the goddess of volcanoes, told her younger sister, Laka, to dance. Laka is now known as the goddess of song and dance and as the patroness of hula dancers. Today, the hula is studied and practiced by people from many different cultures.

Because of Hawaii's isolation, many of its plants and birds and insects are found nowhere else on earth. Sadly, many of them today are on the U.S. endangered species list.

Discover the facts
behind the fiction!

Do you love the *real* things you find
out in the Magic Tree House books?
Join Jack and Annie as they share all the
great research they've done about the
cool places they've been in the

MAGIC TREE HOUSE®
RESEARCH GUIDES

The must-have companions for your favorite
Magic Tree House adventures!

Where have *you* traveled in the
MAGIC TREE HOUSE®?

#1–4: The Mystery of the Tree House*

☐ **#1 DINOSAURS BEFORE DARK** Jack and Annie find the tree house and travel to the time of dinosaurs.

☐ **#2 THE KNIGHT AT DAWN** Jack and Annie go to the time of knights and explore a castle.

☐ **#3 MUMMIES IN THE MORNING** Jack and Annie go to ancient Egypt and get lost in a pyramid while helping a ghost queen.

☐ **#4 PIRATES PAST NOON** Jack and Annie travel back in time and meet pirates with a treasure map.

#5–8: The Mystery of the Magic Spell*

☐ **#5 NIGHT OF THE NINJAS** Jack and Annie go to old Japan and learn the secrets of the ninjas.

☐ **#6 AFTERNOON ON THE AMAZON** Jack and Annie go to the Amazon rain forest and are greeted by army ants, crocodiles, and flesh-eating piranhas.

☐ **#7 SUNSET OF THE SABERTOOTH** Jack and Annie go back

to the Ice Age—the world of woolly mammoths, sabertooth tigers, and a mysterious sorcerer.

☐ **#8 MIDNIGHT ON THE MOON** Jack and Annie go *forward* in time and explore the moon.

#9–12: The Mystery of the Ancient Riddles*

☐ **#9 DOLPHINS AT DAYBREAK** Jack and Annie take a mini-submarine into the world of sharks and dolphins.

☐ **#10 GHOST TOWN AT SUNDOWN** Jack and Annie travel to the Wild West, where they battle horse thieves, meet a kindly cowboy, and get help from a ghost.

☐ **#11 LIONS AT LUNCHTIME** Jack and Annie go to the plains of Africa, where they help wild animals cross a rushing river and have a picnic with a Masai warrior.

☐ **#12 POLAR BEARS PAST BEDTIME** Jack and Annie go to the Arctic, where they meet a seal hunter, play with polar bear cubs, and get trapped on thin ice.

#13–16: The Mystery of the Lost Stories*

☐ **#13 VACATION UNDER THE VOLCANO** Jack and Annie land in Pompeii during Roman times, on the very day Mount Vesuvius erupts!

in time to the War Between the States and help a famous nurse named Clara Barton.

❏ **#22 REVOLUTIONARY WAR ON WEDNESDAY** Jack and Annie go to the shores of the Delaware River the night George Washington and his troops prepare for their famous crossing!

❏ **#23 TWISTER ON TUESDAY** Jack and Annie help save students in a frontier schoolhouse when a tornado hits.

❏ **#24 EARTHQUAKE IN THE EARLY MORNING** Jack and Annie go to San Francisco in 1906—just as the famous earthquake is shaking things up!

#25–28: The Mystery of Morgan's Rhymes

❏ **#25 STAGE FRIGHT ON A SUMMER NIGHT** Jack and Annie travel to Elizabethan England and help William Shakespeare put on a play.

❏ **#26 GOOD MORNING, GORILLAS** Jack and Annie go to the mountains of Africa and meet a family of gorillas!

❏ **#27 THANKSGIVING ON THURSDAY** Jack and Annie meet the Pilgrims and help celebrate the first Thanksgiving.

P. Coughlin/J. Dratfield: Petography, Inc.

About the Author

Mary Pope Osborne is the award-winning author of over fifty books for young people, including *American Tall Tales, Favorite Greek Myths*, the *Spider Kane* mystery books, and *One World, Many Religions*, an Orbis Pictus Honor Book. She recently completed two terms as president of the Authors Guild, the leading writers' organization in the United States. She lives in New York City and Connecticut with her husband, Will, and their Norfolk terrier, Bailey.

Available Now

Magic Tree House #29
(A Merlin Mission)
Christmas in Camelot,

in which Jack and Annie have to find the Water of Memory and Imagination, which will save Camelot from disappearing!

ALSO ON AUDIO FROM LISTENING LIBRARY.
Two-cassette package includes
Christmas in Camelot, read by Mary Pope Osborne
*Magic Tree House Research Guide:
Knights and Castles,* read by Will Osborne

Magic Tree House #30
(A Merlin Mission)
Haunted Castle on Hallow's Eve,

in which Jack and Annie brave ghosts and a scary Raven King to save the Diamond of Destiny. They also get back together with an old friend from Magic Tree House Books #9–12. Can you guess who?